A MOUNTAIN TO CLIMB

First Published by Gwasg Carreg Gwalch 2021 as "Mynydd i'w Ddringo"

Gwasg Carreg Gwalch, 12 Iard yr Orsaf, Llanrwst, Dyffryn Conwy, Cymru LL26 0EH.

ISBN: 978-1-84527-898-4

Published with support from the Welsh Books Council.

CYNGOR LLYFRAU CYMRU

Published by Gwasg Carreg Gwalch,
12 Iard yr Orsaf, Llanrwst, Dyffryn Conwy, Cymru LL26 0EH.
Phone: 01492 642031
e-mail: llyfrau@carreg-gwalch.cymru
web: www.carreg-gwalch.cymru

Printed and published in Wales

A MOUNTAIN TO CLIMB

Original poem
Myrddin ap Dafydd

Translation and pictures
Huw Aaron

Off the bus with a hop and a shout.
Year Five have arrived - for our Big Day Out.

The route's been mapped, and the backpacks packed:
A yo-yo, a bow. An app, a cap, a bun.

A mountain ahead, and Mister Ted - the Head - says:

Some had hoped for fog or rain,
Snowdrifts blocking road and lane.

Tornadoes, storms,
or wildfires blazing up the plain.

Anything but this:

Clumpy boots
that slip and stomp

trip over rock
and squelch through
swamp.

A winding path, a cloudless sky
and Mister Ted (the Head), with map held high:

'There's Humpback Hill, our goal today.
What a thrill! UP AND AWAY!

But first: to recap the rules of play...

No litter

No stalling

No climbing

No falling

No running
No playing

No kidding

But something happens on the slope.
Our tiredness makes way for

hope.

The higher we go
The more we grow.

Above the world,
Among the clouds
Our happiness uncurls,
We're proud.

With a shout - and a hop -
We reach the top.

After the trials, breathless smiles.
And views, brand-new, that stretch for miles.

Fully intent on another ascent,
Everyone... is having fun!

Apart from Mister Ted (the Head),

Who has terrible blisters - and is ready for bed.